The Pony and the Missing Dog

Do you love ponies? Be a Pony Pal!

Look for these Pony Pal books:

#1 I Want a Pony
#2 A Pony for Keeps
#3 A Pony in Trouble
#4 Give Me Back My Pony
#5 Pony to the Rescue
#6 Too Many Ponies
#7 Runaway Pony
#8 Good-bye Pony
#9 The Wild Pony
Super Special #1 The Baby Pony
#10 Don't Hurt My Pony
#11 Circus Pony
#12 Keep Out, Pony!
#13 The Girl Who Hated Ponies
#14 Pony-Sitters
Super Special #2 The Story of Our Ponies
#15 The Blind Pony
#16 The Missing Pony Pal
Super Special #3 The Ghost Pony
#17 Detective Pony
#18 The Saddest Pony
#19 Moving Pony
#20 Stolen Ponies
#21 The Winning Pony
#22 Western Pony
#23 The Pony and the Bear
#24 The Unlucky Pony
#25 The Lonely Pony
#26 The Movie Star Pony

Coming soon

#28 The Newborn Pony

The Pony and the Missing Dog

Jeanne Betancourt

illustrated by Paul Bachem

SCHOLASTIC INC.
New York Toronto London Auckland Sydney
Mexico City New Delhi Hong Kong

ISBN 0-439-21639-7

12 11 10 9 8 7 6 5 4 3 2 1 0/0 1 2 3 4 5/0

Printed in the U.S.A.
First Scholastic printing, September 2000

Contents

The Pony and the Missing Dog

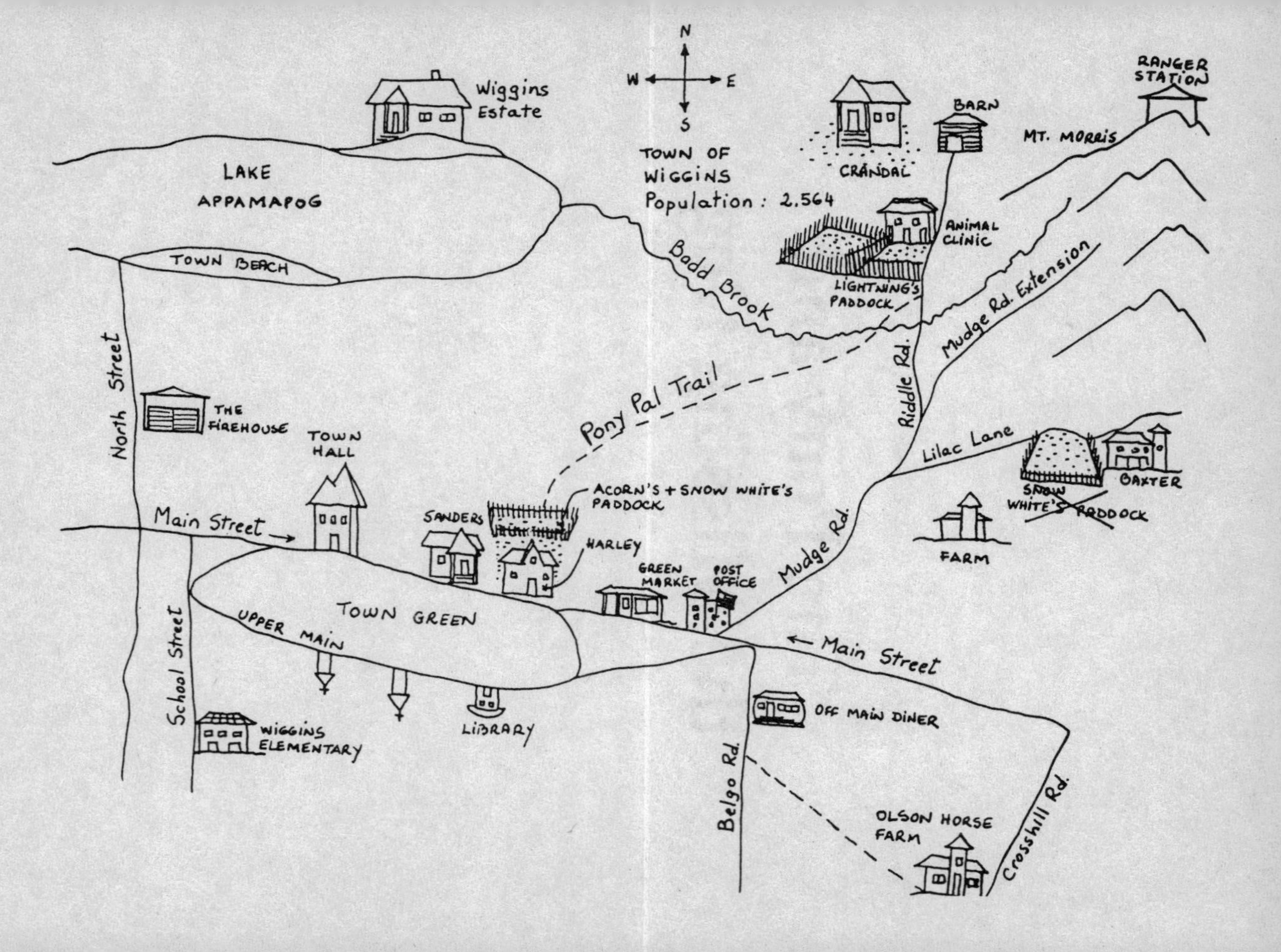
N
W
E
S
TOWN OF
WIGGINS
Population : 2,564
Wiggins
Estate
LAKE
APPAMAPOG
TOWN BEACH
CRANDAL
BARN
RANGER
STATION
MT. MORRIS
ANIMAL
CLINIC
LIGHTNING'S
PADDOCK
Badd Brook
Mudge Rd. Extension
Riddle Rd.
Pony Pal Trail
North Street
THE
FIREHOUSE
TOWN
HALL
Lilac Lane
BAXTER
SNOW
WHITE'S PADDOCK
FARM
ACORN'S + SNOW WHITE'S
PADDOCK
SANDERS
HARLEY
Main Street
Mudge Rd.
GREEN
MARKET
POST
OFFICE
TOWN GREEN
UPPER MAIN
Main Street
School Street
WIGGINS
ELEMENTARY
LIBRARY
OFF MAIN DINER
Belgo Rd.
OLSON HORSE
FARM
Crosshill Rd.

The Rescue

Pam Crandal looked around the big barn. There was fresh straw in all the stalls and the aisles were swept clean. Her barn chores were done. At last she could brush Lightning and saddle her up for a trail ride.

Pam grabbed a currycomb and a grooming brush and left the barn.

Lightning was resting under the sugar maple tree in the middle of the paddock. Her reddish-brown coat was shiny under the morning sun. "Hey, Lightning," Pam called out. "Come on. We're going on a trail ride with our Pony Pals!"

Lightning whinnied as if to say, "Okay," and walked toward Pam.

Suddenly, the Crandals' dog, Woolie, ran out of the barn and under the paddock fence.

"Woolie, no!" shouted Pam.

But it was too late. Woolie was already running toward Lightning.

Woolie was a sheepdog. A sheepdog's instinct is to round up other animals. So when Pam called Lightning, Woolie thought it was his job to get her.

Lightning didn't like Woolie bossing her around. She kicked up her heels and ran to the other side of the paddock. Woolie ran after her. Soon they were playing a game of chase.

I'll never get Lightning now, thought Pam.

Pam remembered that she was baby-sitting her five-year-old brother and sister, Jack and Jill. Pam's parents were on a business trip. Pam and the baby-sitter, Mrs. Bell, were taking care of the twins. Jack and Jill were playing in the field a minute ago, thought Pam. Now where are they?

Finally, Pam saw Jack and Jill coming out of the woods. She ran toward them. I have to tell them that they can't go into the woods alone, she thought. Especially when Mom and Dad aren't here.

Pam noticed that Jack was carrying an animal. Is that a foal? she wondered. A baby pony? As she came closer, she saw that it wasn't a foal. It was a fawn. A baby deer. The smallest deer Pam had ever seen.

"What are you guys doing?" asked Pam. "Where did you find that fawn?"

"It's a baby deer," Jack told Pam in a quiet voice.

"We found him in the woods," added Jill. "He doesn't have a mother."

The fawn had little cream-colored spots on his golden-brown back. He looked up at Pam with big calm eyes.

"He's not afraid of us," whispered Jack.

"How do you know the mother deer isn't looking for her baby?" asked Pam.

"She isn't," said Jill. "We waited a *very* long time and she didn't come. She left her baby all alone."

"You couldn't have waited a *very* long time," Pam told them. "I just saw you in the barn a little while ago."

Jack and Jill pretended they hadn't heard what Pam said.

"I think a hunter killed the mother," said Jack excitedly.

"So we have to be the mother," added Jill. "We have to take care of him."

"The first thing you have to do is put him down," said Pam.

"He was lying in the woods," said Jill. "He can't stand."

"He was probably resting when you found him," explained Pam. "Deer are like ponies. They stand right after they are born. So he can stand. Now put him down."

Jack lowered his arms. The fawn stuck

out his four skinny legs. When the fawn's hooves hit the ground, Jack let go. The fawn wobbled back and forth.

"He's going to fall," cried Jack. "We have to pick him up again."

"Leave him alone," insisted Pam. "That's how fawns walk at first. Just like foals."

The fawn made a little bleating noise.

"He's crying," said Jill.

"He wants his mother's milk," explained Pam.

Jill grabbed Pam's hand and pulled on it. "We have to feed him with a bottle," she said. "Like a baby."

The fawn took a few wobbly steps toward the woods.

"And make a house for him," said Jack. "So he doesn't run away."

Pam sighed. The twins didn't understand that the fawn wasn't a pet.

Pam saw a flash of golden hair coming toward them. It was Woolie!

Before Pam could stop him, Woolie was barking and running circles around the

fawn. The little fawn shook with terror and made a frightened, squeaky noise. Pam knew that Woolie was trying to herd the fawn. But she was still angry with her dog.

Pam grabbed Woolie's collar and pulled him away from the fawn. "Stop it!" she hissed in Woolie's ear. "Bad dog."

"Bad dog," scolded Jill.

"Sit, Woolie," commanded Pam.

Woolie sat. His ears went back and a sad look came into his eyes.

"Now stay," Pam told him. She turned to her brother. "You hold on to Woolie's collar, Jack," Pam ordered. "I have to figure out what to do with this fawn. We have to find his mother."

The fawn took another few steps.

"I told you he doesn't have a mother," wailed Jill. "I'm his mother now."

"Dad and Mom would let us keep him," Jack told Pam. "You're a meanie."

"Stop it, both of you," Pam told the twins.

She wished her Pony Pals — Anna and

Lulu — were there. Together they could figure out what to do.

Pam was supposed to meet them on Pony Pal Trail. Pony Pal Trail went a mile and a half through the woods. It connected Acorn and Snow White's paddock with the Crandals' property.

Pam looked at her watch. It was almost ten-thirty. She was already fifteen minutes late.

"We *have to* feed our baby deer," insisted Jill. "We have to get some milk and a bottle and feed him."

"If we don't pick him up, Pam, he'll run away and be lost forever," whined Jack.

Woolie whimpered as if to say, "Why can't I round up that little fellow? I'll put him in the paddock with Lightning. It's my job."

The fawn looked at Pam as if to say, "Where's my mother?"

Pam didn't know what to do.

At that instant, Anna burst off Pony Pal Trail into the Crandals' big field. She was riding her brown-and-black Shetland pony, Acorn.

A rider on a beautiful white pony followed Anna and Acorn out of the woods. It was Lulu on Snow White.

Could the Pony Pals figure out if the fawn really was an orphan? Should they try to feed the fawn with a bottle? Or should they put him back in the woods?

Pam hoped with all her heart that her Pony Pals would know what to do.

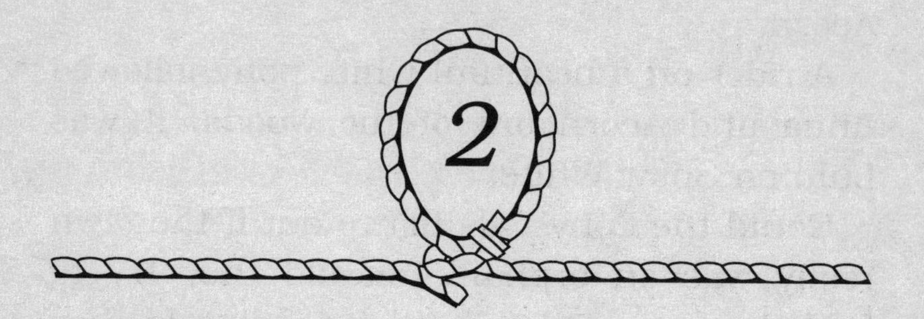

Alone in the Woods

Anna and Lulu rode across the field toward Pam and the twins. The fawn lay down.

Acorn and Snow White will look big and scary to the fawn, thought Pam. She put her hand up to signal Anna and Lulu to stop. The two girls halted their ponies and dismounted. Jill ran over to tell them about the fawn.

Woolie pulled to get away from Jack. "Woolie wants to go say hi to everybody," Jack told Pam.

"But he can't," said Pam. "It will frighten the fawn."

Anna and Lulu tied their ponies to the hitching post. Then they came over to see the fawn for themselves. The fawn looked up at all the people standing around him. But he didn't try to stand up again.

He must wonder when his mother is coming, thought Pam.

"Oh, my," whispered Lulu. "This is a very young fawn."

"We saw a doe in the woods," Anna said. "Maybe she was his mother."

"She left him alone," said Jack.

"Just a baby, all by himself," added Jill.

"There's something you don't know about mother deer and their fawns," Lulu told the twins. "The mothers leave their babies alone during the day. While the baby rests, the mother goes around looking for things to eat. Otherwise, she can't make milk for her baby. The mother of this fawn might be looking for him right now."

"What if the deer you saw was another deer?" asked Jack. "And this fawn's mother is dead? Then we'd *have to* keep him."

"It's not even hunting season, Jack," said Anna.

Anna bent down and looked in the fawn's eyes. "You're so darling," she said. "You're the most beautiful little thing in the world."

The fawn made another bleating noise.

"He's hungry!" exclaimed Jill. "I want to give him a bottle."

"No!" scolded Pam.

"There shouldn't be any more people smells on him," Lulu explained to Jill. "A mother deer knows what her baby smells like. We want her to recognize the smell of her son. Otherwise, she might reject him. We should take him to the woods right now."

Tears streamed down Jill's face. "He's mine," she cried. "I'm supposed to take care of him. I already love him."

Pam put a hand on her sister's shoulder. "If you love him, you want him to be with his mommy," she said. "Right?"

Jill nodded.

"Do you guys think you can remember where you found him?" Lulu asked the twins.

"I do," said Jill. "I'll carry him. It's my turn. Jack already did."

"A fawn is like a baby pony," Lulu told Jill. "Pam is the most experienced with baby ponies. So she should carry him."

"Jill, you can show me the way," said Pam. "Jack's job is to keep Woolie from following us."

Pam lifted up the fawn. He was light in her arms and warm. He turned his little head and looked up at her. He isn't afraid, she thought. He trusts me.

"Let's go," Pam told Jill.

Jill led the way into the woods. As Pam walked she felt the fawn's heart thumping gently against her arm. "We're bringing you back to your mama," she whispered.

Pam thought how lucky she was that Lulu Sanders was a Pony Pal. Lulu knew what to do about the fawn. And she was smart about

a lot of wild animals, not just fawns. Lulu's father was a naturalist who went all over the world to study animals. Before Lulu moved to Wiggins, she traveled with her father. Her mother died when Lulu was little. Now Lulu lived with her grandmother in a house right next to Anna's. Lulu missed her dad, but she loved being in Wiggins with her friends and her pony, Snow White. Pam hadn't known Lulu for a long time. But it felt like they'd been friends forever.

Pam and Anna Harley had been best friends since kindergarten. They both loved ponies, being outdoors, and having a good time. The only thing they disagreed about was schoolwork. Pam loved to read and write and do math problems. But Anna was dyslexic, so those subjects were difficult for her. Anna's talent was in art. She loved to draw and paint. Pam had a big painting of Lightning hanging in her bedroom. It was an Anna Harley original.

Pam Crandal had always had a pony of her own. Pam's father was a veterinarian and her mother was a horseback-riding instructor. There were a lot of horses and ponies at the Crandals'. Pam had taken care of baby ponies. But she had never carried a newborn fawn.

Jill led Pam over to a clump of bushes and pointed to a small pile of twigs. "There," she said. "He was lying there."

Pam gently lowered the fawn onto the pile of brambles.

Jill put her hand out to pet the little fawn.

"Don't touch him, Jill," whispered Pam. "Remember, we want his mother to recognize his smell. Your smell could cover it up."

Pam knew how Jill felt. She wanted to pet the fawn, too.

Pam took Jill's hand. "Come on," she told her sister. "Let's go."

"Bye, fawn," whispered Jill. "I hope your mommy finds you."

The sisters ran quietly along the path that led out of the woods.

Behind them they heard the fawn's sad bleat.

"He's calling us, Pam," Jill said. "We have to go back."

"He's calling his mother," Pam explained.

Pam saw a deer run across the trail ahead of them.

Will the mother deer come back for her baby? Pam wondered. If she does, will she love him and feed him? Or will she reject him because humans touched him?

Anna, Lulu, and Jack were waiting for Pam and Jill.

"We put the fawn back," Jill told them. "And Pam saw a deer in the woods."

Pam looked around. She didn't see Woolie anywhere. Did he go into the woods to look for the fawn? Was Woolie causing more trouble?

Where's Woolie?

"Where's Woolie?" Pam asked Jack. "You were supposed to keep him from following us."

"He didn't follow you," said Jack.

"He's keeping an eye on the ponies," Lulu told Pam. She pointed toward the paddock. "Look."

Pam saw three ponies grazing near one another. Woolie was running in a circle around them.

"He thinks he's making them stay together," said Lulu. "He's pretending they're sheep."

"Can we go on our trail ride now?" asked Anna.

"Let's," agreed Pam. She told the twins that they should go back to the house. "Mrs. Bell will watch you now," she said.

"What about the fawn?" Jill asked the Pony Pals. "What if his mother doesn't come back?"

"We'll check on him when we start our trail ride," Lulu promised.

Anna reached into her pocket and handed Jack a brown bag. "Here are some brownies for you guys and Mrs. Bell," she said. Anna's mother owned a diner and made the best brownies ever.

"I brought some for the trail ride, too," Anna told Pam and Lulu.

Pam held out the Pony Pal whistle she wore around her neck. "If the fawn is gone, I'll make four long blasts on my whistle," she explained to the twins. "Stay on the porch so you can hear."

Fifteen minutes later the Pony Pals were finally ready to go. Pam had the first aid kit and snacks for the ponies in her saddlebags. Lulu had binoculars, a camera, a flashlight, and a book to identify animal tracks.

Sandwiches, brownies, a drawing pad, and pencils were in Anna's saddlebags.

Each of the Pony Pals also had an extra sweater and water.

Pam swung into her saddle. "Let's ride!" she shouted.

Anna and Lulu mounted and the riders turned their ponies toward Pony Pal Trail. Suddenly, Woolie was barking and running under the ponies. The startled ponies snorted, shifted, and bumped into one another.

"Woolie, stop it!" Pam shouted.

Woolie was so excited that he couldn't stop.

"He wants to go on the trail ride," said Lulu.

"Let him come," said Anna. "He always has fun with us."

"He's been nothing but trouble all day," said Pam. "Look how he's misbehaving."

Lulu straightened out Snow White. "Woolie's still excited because of the fawn."

"That's another reason he can't come with us," said Pam. "He'll be looking for the fawn."

Woolie barked. Acorn spooked and Anna almost fell off.

Pam jumped off Lightning. "I'm putting you inside," she told Woolie.

Pam unhooked Lightning's lead rope, clipped it to Woolie's collar, and led him to the house.

A few minutes later the Pony Pals began their ride. They moved their ponies at a slow walk and didn't talk. They were headed toward the spot where Pam had left the fawn. Pam was the first to notice that the fawn wasn't there.

The girls stayed perfectly still and looked around. Lulu pointed into the woods. Pam saw a doe half hidden by a tree trunk. The fawn was right beside his mother.

Lulu carefully reached into her saddlebag,

took out her camera, and snapped a photo. Acorn nickered.

The mother deer made a warning sound to her fawn. She turned and quickly ran deeper into the woods. The fawn followed her.

"I'll give Jack and Jill the photo of the fawn with his mother," Lulu told Pam.

Pam smiled at Lulu. "Thanks." She blew her whistle four times.

The Pony Pals turned their ponies toward Ms. Wiggins's estate. Ms. Wiggins had super trails and let the girls ride there whenever they wanted.

"Let's practice jumping in the field with rock walls," suggested Anna.

"Then have lunch at our favorite spot by Badd Brook," added Lulu.

Lightning turned in a small circle. "He already wants to jump," laughed Pam.

After an hour of riding and jumping, the Pony Pals and their ponies were ready for a rest. The ponies drank from Badd Brook. The girls sat on the rocks and Anna unpacked their lunch.

"I'm so glad Woolie isn't here," said Pam. "He'd have driven us crazy when we were jumping."

"He doesn't always bother the ponies," said Anna. She handed Pam a sandwich. "Sometimes he goes off and has his own adventures."

"He's a great dog," commented Lulu. "And the ponies really like him."

"Well, he was getting on my nerves today," said Pam.

"Let's play with him when we get back," suggested Lulu. "In case his feelings are hurt."

"We'll pretend we're sheep and he can try to herd us," giggled Anna.

Pam was glad that her friends liked Woolie. But she was still a little mad at him.

The Pony Pals rode some more after lunch. They stopped at Ms. Wiggins's house before going home. Ms. Wiggins was very interested in the story about the fawn. "You did the right thing," she said.

Ms. Wiggins told the Pony Pals that someone was putting animal traps on her land illegally. "I'm trying to get rid of all those traps," she added.

"I hope the fawn doesn't get caught in one," said Anna. "He had enough excitement today for a whole lifetime."

"Do you girls want to stay for dinner?" asked Ms. Wiggins.

"We're having a barn sleepover at Pam's," Lulu told Ms. Wiggins. "Mrs. Bell is making us dinner."

They said good-bye to Ms. Wiggins and started the long ride back to the Crandals'.

As Pam rode along the trail, she thought about Woolie. I really was mean to him, she told herself. He didn't do anything wrong. He was just following his instinct to herd animals.

Pam decided that when she got home, she'd tell Woolie that she was sorry. She'd hug him, scratch behind his ears, and give him a big bone.

The sun was setting when the girls rode up to the Crandal barn. They took off their ponies' saddles and wiped down the ponies with cool water.

Pam called out Woolie's name. But he didn't come.

"We'll water and feed Lightning for you," offered Lulu. "You can go look for Woolie."

Pam ran through the old barn and the new barn, calling Woolie's name and looking for him.

No Woolie.

Next she went to the house. When she opened the kitchen door, she called out, "Woolie! Come here, Woolie."

She waited. Then called again.

Mrs. Bell came into the kitchen. "Woolie isn't in the house, dear," she said. "I let him out a couple of hours ago."

Pam went to the playroom where Jack and Jill were playing on the computer.

"Have you seen Woolie?" Pam asked the twins.

Jill shook her head. "Me neither," said Jack.

"Tell us about the fawn," pleaded Jill.

Pam quickly told them about the fawn and his mother. "Lulu took a picture for you," she added. "Now, let's go. We have to find Woolie."

The Pony Pals and the twins looked all over the Crandal property for Woolie.

"He's probably wandering around the woods," said Pam. "He does that a lot. He'll come back when he's hungry." She looked at her watch. It was six-thirty. "He should be hungry by now."

"Dinner's ready!" Mrs. Bell called from the house.

After dinner the Pony Pals went along the edge of the woods. They each carried a flashlight and called out Woolie's name.

Still no Woolie.

It was too late to go into the woods to look for him.

"Maybe he didn't even go into the woods," suggested Lulu.

"Wherever he went, it's too late to look now," added Anna.

"I know," said Pam sadly.

At nine o'clock the Pony Pals went to the hayloft and laid their sleeping bags out on the floor. They crawled into their bags and talked. They talked a little bit about the fawn, but mostly they talked about Woolie.

"I bet he'll be here when we get up tomorrow," said Anna. "He'll probably wake us up with his barking."

"I hope so," said Pam.

"Don't worry, Pam," Lulu said. "Woolie is a smart dog. He can take care of himself."

Soon Anna and Lulu were asleep.

But Pam lay awake. She looked out the hayloft window at the starry sky. Where are you, Woolie? she wondered. Where are you?

Tracking

Pam woke up during the night. She listened to rain splattering on the barn roof and worried about Woolie.

Was he lost in the woods? Was he wet and shivering? Was he hurt?

When the rain stopped, Pam heard something moving around in the barn. Maybe that's him, she thought. She crawled out of her sleeping bag and went down the hayloft ladder. But the noise was Fat Cat chasing a mouse.

Pam looked up at the barn clock. It was

five in the morning. The sun will rise in an hour, she thought. I'll do my barn chores now. Then we can have an early start searching for Woolie.

Pam quickly dressed, fed her mother's horses and ponies, and cleaned out the stalls. After that she went out to the paddock to feed Lightning, Acorn, and Snow White.

Next she went to the house. She made cheese sandwiches, put juice in a thermos, took six apples from the fruit bowl, and wrote a note to Mrs. Bell and the twins.

Mrs. Bell, Jack, and Jill,
Woolie is still missing. We left early to search for him. Maybe Woolie will come back while we're gone. I hope so.
Love, Pam
P.S. Jack and Jill, do not go in the woods alone again. For any reason. Mrs. Bell is in charge of you.

Pam put the note on the table. As she was leaving the kitchen she remembered to pack two more things — Woolie's water bowl and dog biscuits.

Back in the hayloft, Pam woke up Anna and Lulu. "Woolie's not back," she told them.

Anna rubbed the sleep out of her eyes. "He's never stayed away this long," she said.

"He always comes back by morning," added Lulu.

"Maybe he tried to follow us yesterday and lost his way," said Anna.

"Or is injured," Pam said. "Or is — " Her eyes filled up with tears. She couldn't say what she was thinking.

Lulu was already out of her sleeping bag and dressed. "Let's try to search for him," she said. "We'll look for clues."

"Like his tracks," said Anna. She was getting dressed now, too.

"We'll blow our whistles and call his name," added Pam. "If he's in trouble, he'll bark. Then we can rescue him."

While the girls were saddling up the ponies, they talked more about how to find Woolie.

"We should start on Pony Pal Trail," suggested Lulu. "If he was trying to follow us, that's where he'd go. He'd follow our scent."

The three riders led their ponies onto the trail. "I'll go first," suggested Lulu, "to look for tracks."

"It rained last night," said Pam. "That would wash away tracks."

"You said it didn't rain for very long," Lulu reminded Pam. She pointed a few feet ahead of her. "There's one of our pony's tracks from yesterday. So we might find Woolie's tracks. It's worth a try."

"And we should look for dog scat," suggested Anna. "It looks a lot different from a pony plop."

The girls walked carefully along the trail. Pam saw what looked like a dog track. She called Lulu to come check it out.

Lulu bent over the track and studied it.

“That’s a raccoon track,” Lulu explained. “See the long nails? And Woolie’s track has more padding between the toes. I remember noticing that when we played with him in the snow.”

“Woolie doesn’t always stay on the trail,” said Pam. “We have to spread out.” She felt discouraged. The woods were so big. How were they ever going to find one little dog?

“I’ll watch the ponies,” suggested Anna. “Pam, you and Lulu can go into the woods beside the trail.”

Pam and Lulu agreed that was a good idea.

“Blow one long blast on your whistle for calling Woolie,” said Lulu. “Use two short blasts if you find a clue.”

Pam pushed her way through the underbrush on the right side of the trail. “Woolie,” she called. "Woolie, where are you?" She blew a long blast on her whistle. Then she listened for an answering bark. There was none.

After a little way, Pam came to a barbed wire fence. Woolie has lots of fluffy hair, she thought. His hair could get caught in the barbs. Pam walked slowly along the fence looking for strands of Woolie's hair. Finally, she found what she was looking for — little tufts of golden-white hair caught in the barbed wire.

Pam blew two short blasts on her whistle.

In a few minutes Lulu was by her side. Lulu carefully removed the hair. "Woolie's fur is much softer than this," she said. "I think this hair is from a deer's tail."

Pam felt the hairs between her fingers. Lulu was right. The strands were thicker and stiffer than Woolie's hair.

Pam and Lulu went back to Anna and the ponies on the trail. The girls rode for a while. They called out Woolie's name and blew their whistles. But Woolie didn't bark an answer.

The ponies didn't startle at the shrill sound of the whistles. And they were extra responsive to their riders' commands. Acorn, Snow White, and Lightning knew that they were on a Pony Pal mission.

Suddenly, Pam had a horrible feeling in the pit of her stomach and tears sprang to her eyes. What if Woolie hadn't tried to follow them? What if he had run away?

The Runaway

Pam halted Lightning in the middle of Pony Pal Trail.

Lulu and Anna pulled their ponies up beside them.

"Pam, why did you stop?" asked Lulu. "Did you hear something?"

"No," answered Pam. "I just had an idea about Woolie. I don't think he came this way."

"He wanted to follow us, Pam," said Anna. "So he picked up our scent and followed us onto Pony Pal Trail."

"I don't think Woolie was trying to follow us," said Pam. "I think he went in a whole other direction. I think he ran away."

Pam couldn't stop the tears anymore. They streamed down her cheeks.

"We'd better have an emergency Pony Pal meeting," said Lulu.

"Come on, Pam," suggested Anna. "We'll stop right here and think about what to do next."

The Pony Pals dismounted and sat against trees at the edge of the trail.

"Why do you think Woolie ran away?" Lulu asked.

"Because I was so mean to him," answered Pam.

"You weren't mean," said Anna. "You just put him in the house when we went on a trail ride. You've done that before."

"But I was angry at him when I did it," explained Pam.

"He wouldn't run away because you were a little angry at him," insisted Lulu. "Woolie's a sweet, forgiving dog."

"I know he is," said Pam. Tears sprang to her eyes again. "But I yelled at him two other times before you came."

"Why?" asked Anna. "What'd he do?"

"First he was trying to herd Lightning when I wanted to saddle her up. I yelled at him for that. Then, when the twins brought the fawn out of the woods, Woolie barked and scared him. So I scolded Woolie again. I told him he was a bad dog. I really hurt his feelings. I could see it in his eyes."

"Pam, even if he did run away, he'll come back," said Lulu. "Or we'll find him."

Anna put her arm around Pam. "Then you can tell him you're sorry," she said. "And everything will go back to normal."

"But what if we *don't* find him?" insisted Pam. "I may never see him again."

Anna handed Pam a tissue.

Lulu stood in front of Pam. "Pam," she said, "do you want to find Woolie?"

"Yes," sobbed Pam. "Of course I do."

"Then you can't sit here crying," Lulu told her. "You have to do something. There are

two possibilities: One, Woolie tried to follow us. Two, Woolie ran away. Now what are we going to do to find him?"

"I have an idea," said Anna. "Let's make posters and put them up all over town. Whether he ran away or got lost, he's still a missing dog."

"That's a great idea," said Lulu. "And Pam, you should call your neighbors and ask if they've seen Woolie."

The girls remounted their ponies.

"Did Woolie have his collar on?" Anna asked.

"Yes," answered Pam. "It's a red collar with his name and our address on it."

"Good," said Anna as she swung into the saddle. "If someone finds him they'll know who to call."

Lulu mounted Snow White. "Okay," she said. "Let's go make some posters and phone calls."

As they rode onto Pony Pal Trail, Lulu pulled up beside Pam. "It'll be okay, Pam," she said. "We'll find him."

Pam knew that Lulu was trying to make her feel better. But nothing could change the way she felt. Her dog was missing. He could be injured or dead. She might never see him again. And it was all her fault.

When the Pony Pals reached the Crandals' big open field, Pam looked in all directions. She hoped with all her heart that Woolie had come home while they were gone.

But Woolie wasn't there.

The three girls went into the barn office. Anna did a drawing of Woolie and Lulu wrote the words underneath.

They made several copies of the poster on Mrs. Crandal's photocopy machine.

At the same time, Pam made phone calls. First she called Ms. Wiggins. Next she called her neighbors on Riddle Road and Mudge Road Extension. No one had seen Woolie.

"No luck," reported Pam.

"We can't give up," Anna told Pam.

Pam knew that Anna was right. But in her heart she already had given up. She was scared she would never see Woolie again.

Missing Dog

MEDIUM SIZED DOG. GOLDEN COLOR
Red collar with I.D.

IF FOUND please call:
555-4362

Red Collar

Lulu yanked on Pam's shirtsleeve. "Hey," she said. "Don't think sad thoughts about Woolie. Think about how to find him."

"Think hard, Pam," said Anna. "Did you call everybody who lives around here? Is there anyone you forgot to call?"

Pam drew a map of Riddle Road and Mudge Road Extension in her mind. She pictured the houses and farms on these roads.

"The Quinns," Pam said finally. "I didn't call the Quinns. They live on Mudge Road

Extension. Woolie might have gone that way."

Pam looked up the Quinns' telephone number and called them.

Mrs. Quinn answered the phone. She liked the Pony Pals and was happy to hear Pam's voice.

Pam asked Mrs. Quinn if she'd seen a small blond sheepdog in the last twenty-four hours. "He has fluffy blond hair and a red collar," Pam added.

"We did see a dog like that," said Mrs. Quinn.

"You did!" exclaimed Pam.

"He was chasing the kitten you gave us," Mrs. Quinn said. "And he tried to chase our old pony, Ginger."

"That sounds just like Woolie," said Pam excitedly. "Is he still there?"

"This all happened yesterday," explained Mrs. Quinn. "He ran off after a while."

Woolie was at the Quinns' *yesterday*, thought Pam. A lot could have happened in twenty-four hours.

"Did you say your dog had a collar, Pam?" asked Mrs. Quinn.

"A red one," Pam reminded her.

"Well, this dog didn't have a collar," Mrs. Quinn said.

If the dog didn't have a collar it wasn't Woolie, thought Pam. She thanked Mrs. Quinn and hung up the phone.

Pam told Anna and Lulu that Mrs. Quinn had seen a dog that looked like Woolie. "But he didn't have a collar."

"It could still be Woolie," said Lulu. "Woolie could have lost his collar. Maybe it was caught on a fence."

"Or he swam in the brook and it slipped off," said Anna.

"You're right," said Pam. "I didn't think of that."

"Let's go over to the Quinns' right away," suggested Anna.

"We'll ask them some more questions and look for clues," added Lulu. "And we'll try to track Woolie from there."

Pam picked up a marker and wrote *Might*

not have collar on all the posters they made.

The twins came running into the office. Mrs. Bell was right behind them. "Did you find Woolie?" asked Jack.

"Not yet," answered Pam. "But we have a lead and we made these posters."

Pam held up a poster for Mrs. Bell and the twins to see.

"I want to help find Woolie, too," said Jill. "I miss him."

"What can we do to help, Pam?" asked Mrs. Bell.

"You could take the posters to town and put them up," answered Pam.

"We'll put one in the diner," said Jack.

"And on the big bulletin board in the Green Market," added Jill.

Mrs. Bell picked up the pile of posters. "We'll go do it right now," she told Pam.

"And we'll continue our search," said Pam.

A few minutes later, the three girls rode their ponies onto Riddle Road. Pam led the way to Mudge Road Extension. As they rode, Pam called out Woolie's name and blew her whistle. But no barks answered her call.

The girls rode their ponies right up to the Quinns' house. Mr. and Mrs. Quinn were sitting on the front porch. The Quinns both liked ponies very much. As the girls dismounted, Mrs. Quinn came over and patted each pony on the head.

After the girls said hello to the Quinns, Lulu started the interview.

"We want to ask you some questions about that dog," she began. "We think it might be Woolie and that he lost his collar."

Pam took out a photo of Woolie and showed it to the Quinns. They both agreed that it looked exactly like the dog they saw.

"You told Pam the dog ran off," Lulu said. "Did either of you see where he went?"

"I did," answered Mr. Quinn. He pointed to a row of pine trees near the pony shed. "He went into the field behind those trees. Right about in the middle of that row."

"That's a big clue, Mr. Quinn," said Lulu. "Thank you."

The Pony Pals said good-bye to the

Quinns. As they passed the paddock they gave Ginger an apple. The kitten, Pal, came over and rubbed against Pam's leg. Pam picked up Pal and kissed his little face. "We have to go find Woolie," she told the kitten as she put him down.

Pal jumped up on Ginger's back and lay down there. Ginger looked over her shoulder and knickered a greeting to the kitten.

"Ginger is Pal's couch," laughed Anna.

The girls led their ponies to the row of pine trees.

"You go first, Lulu," suggested Pam. "You're best at finding clues."

Lulu and Snow White led the way between two pine trees into the field.

Lulu hunched over to look for tracks. "There's so much grass it's hard to find tracks," she said.

Lightning pulled on her reins to go right.

Pam loosened her grip. Lightning headed toward a large bush on the edge of the field.

"Lightning," said Pam, "are you looking for a clue or for a snack of leaves?"

Lightning sniffed the bush. Pam noticed that the bush had lots of thorns. She knew Lightning wouldn't eat that. Did Lightning find a clue? wondered Pam.

Pam went up to the bush. She thought she saw a bunny. But when she came closer she saw it wasn't a bunny. It was a tuft of golden fur caught on the thorny bush.

Pam carefully took the hair off the thorns and rubbed it between her fingers. It was fine and soft. Just like Woolie's fur.

Lulu and Anna agreed that the fur looked and felt like Woolie's.

"Good work, Lightning," said Pam.

"Lightning's picked up Woolie's trail," said Lulu. "We should let her lead us."

The three girls and the other two ponies followed Lightning out of the field onto a narrow trail.

As they went along the trail, the girls looked for more clues. But they didn't find any.

After twenty minutes on the trail, they came out on Lilac Lane. The Pony Pals waited to see what Lightning would do next. She poked her nose at Pam's pocket for a treat and nickered as if to say, "Hey, where's my reward?"

"I guess she's finished being a detective for now," said Pam.

Lulu took three carrots out of her saddle-bag for the ponies.

Woolie knows his way all over Wiggins, thought Pam. *He can find his way home. Only two things could keep him away: One, he's injured and can't come home. Or two, he doesn't want to come home. Which one is it?* wondered Pam. *Will we ever know? Will we ever find Woolie?*

7

My Doggie

Pam looked up and down the road. There were houses and farms on both sides.

"Maybe Woolie is hanging around here," said Anna. "He could even be in one of the houses."

"I think we should go to every house and farm and ask," said Pam.

"You and Anna do that," said Lulu. "I'll stay with the ponies and look for more clues on the road."

"I'll check the places on the right side," Pam told Anna. "You take the left."

Pam's first stop was a small blue house. She rang the doorbell.

A young boy opened the door.

"Hi," said Pam. "I'm looking for a missing dog."

Pam looked around for an adult. Through a doorway she saw the corner of a rug. And on the rug she saw the back end of a dog. A blond-haired dog!

A woman came through the door. "We're not buying anything," she said in a grouchy voice. "So go away." She glared at the little boy. "Jimmy, I told you not to open the door to strangers."

"I'm not selling anything," Pam explained. "My name's Pam Crandal. I live on Riddle Road. I lost my dog. I wondered if you saw him." She held up the photo of Woolie. "He looks like this."

"I have a dog," said the little boy. "His name is Doggie. He looks like that dog. But he's *my* dog."

Maybe Jimmy found Woolie, thought Pam.

He calls him Doggie because he doesn't know his name!

"Can I meet your dog?" Pam asked Jimmy.

"Doggie!" Jimmy called. A dog bounded into the hall, his tail wagging. He did look like Woolie, but was almost twice Woolie's size.

Pam reached down and patted Doggie on the head.

"Doggie is very cute," said Pam. "But my dog is smaller." She smiled up at Jimmy's mother. "I'm sorry to bother you."

Jimmy's mother stopped being grouchy. She told Pam that she would keep her eye out for Woolie. "And I'll call your place if I see him," she promised. "We bring Doggie to your father all the time. He's a great vet. I'm sorry he lost his dog."

As Pam walked away from the blue house, she thought about her father and mother. They both loved Woolie as much as she did. And they'd left her in charge of him. Pam felt like crying again, but she remembered Lulu's advice. She shouldn't waste time feeling bad. She had to use all her energy to find Woolie.

Pam's next stop was a big farm. A man was driving a tractor toward a field of corn. She ran to catch up with him. "Excuse me, sir," she shouted above the roar of the tractor.

The driver stopped the tractor and looked down at Pam. "What can I do for you, young lady?" he asked in a friendly voice.

"I'm looking for my dog," Pam told the farmer. "He's been missing since yesterday morning." She showed the man Woolie's picture.

"That dog was hanging around here yesterday," the man said. "I'm sure that's him."

The farmer turned off the tractor engine. "I thought maybe he was a stray because he had no collar," he added.

"He lost his collar," explained Pam. "His name is Woolie. Did he look okay?"

"He looked fine," the farmer said. "He was just hungry. So I fed him."

"Thank you," Pam said. She looked around. "Is he still here?"

"That's the strange thing," the man said. "The dog — your dog — he stayed the night. Slept in the barn. I brought him some more to eat this morning, when I came out to milk the cows."

"So he slept here," said Pam.

The man nodded. "After I milked the cows, I came back to the house for breakfast," he said. "When I came out later, the dog was gone. Just run off. Maybe he had enough adventures and went home."

"Oh, I hope so," said Pam excitedly.

She thanked the farmer and ran all the way back to the road. Lulu and Anna were waiting for her at the end of Lilac Lane.

"Someone saw him!" Pam shouted as she ran toward her friends. She told them everything the farmer had said.

Lightning whinnied excitedly. "Guess what, Lightning," Pam told her pony. "We have another clue."

"We're close to the diner," said Anna. "Let's go there and call your house. Maybe Woolie's already there."

The three girls mounted their ponies and rode to the diner.

Pam listened to the even *clip-clop, clip-clop* of the ponies' hooves. *"Please go home, Woolie,"* Pam whispered to their beat. *"Please go home, Woolie."*

Three Ideas

The Pony Pals tied their ponies to the hitching post and went into the diner. Their missing-dog poster was on the bulletin board near the front door. All the booths were filled, but there were three empty seats at the counter.

Anna sat on a stool. "Why don't you telephone home," she said to Pam. "We'll order lunch. What do you want to eat?"

Pam didn't feel hungry. She was too upset about Woolie. But she knew she would need energy to keep looking for him. Pam told

Anna to order her a grilled cheese sandwich. Then she went to the telephone in the back of the diner.

Mrs. Bell answered the phone. Pam asked her if Woolie was there.

"No, dear," said Mrs. Bell. "We put up all the posters. When we came home we looked for Woolie again. In the barns, paddocks, and fields. He's not here."

Pam told Mrs. Bell that Woolie had stayed at a farm overnight and then disappeared again. "We're going to keep looking for him," said Pam.

Pam went back to the counter. She didn't have to tell the Pony Pals that Woolie was still missing. They could tell just by looking at her.

"It's time for another emergency meeting," said Lulu.

"We need three ideas," said Pam. "And fast."

"While we eat our sandwiches, let's each think of an idea," suggested Anna. "When we finish eating we'll share them."

The girls ate their sandwiches and chips in silence. Lulu wrote something on her paper place mat. Anna drew her idea on the back of a menu.

As Pam took the last bite of her sandwich, she finally had an idea, too. She pulled a little notebook out of her pocket and quickly wrote her idea down.

"Ready for the meeting?" Lulu asked her friends.

Anna nodded.

Pam put down her pencil. "Ready," she said.

"Here's my idea," said Lulu. She tore off a piece of her place mat and handed it to Pam. Pam read it out loud.

“That’s a very good idea,” Anna told Lulu. “Woolie loves it over there. Maybe that’s where he went this morning. There are lots of places to look at Ms. Wiggins’s.”

“What’s your idea, Pam?” asked Lulu.

Pam put her notebook on the counter.

We need more
people to help
search for Woolie.

“We can start by asking Ms. Wiggins to help us,” suggested Pam. “And maybe one of the people who work for her.”

“Here’s my idea,” said Anna. “It’s connected to both of your ideas.”

Anna turned the menu over and they all looked at her drawing.

"I think we should separate when we look for Woolie," said Anna.

"We can do that on Ms. Wiggins's property," suggested Pam. "We know our way all over that place. We can have an organized search and none of us will get lost there."

"Let's call Ms. Wiggins right now," said Lulu.

Anna went to the kitchen to get carrots for the ponies. Lulu cleared away their dishes. And Pam called Ms. Wiggins.

The phone rang. And rang. Please be home, prayed Pam. The Pony Pals need your help.

Finally, on the fifth ring, Ms. Wiggins answered the phone.

Pam told her that they still hadn't found Woolie.

"I'm so sorry," said Ms. Wiggins. "Is there anything I can do to help?"

Pam told Ms. Wiggins that they wanted to do a big search of her land.

"Come right over," said Ms. Wiggins. "I'll join your search party. I'll saddle up Picasso and be ready when you get here."

"That's great," said Pam. "We knew we could count on you."

"Mike Lacey will help, too," added Ms. Wiggins. "He can ride his trail bike."

"Mike!" exclaimed Pam. "He's not a friend of the Pony Pals."

Mike Lacey and Tommy Rand were older than the Pony Pals, but they acted very immature. Mike and Tommy called the Pony Pals the Pony Pests. Once they even stole their ponies. Another time Mike and Tommy set traps for animals on Ms. Wiggins's land. Snow White was caught in one of those traps.

Pam reminded Ms. Wiggins about the terrible things Mike and Tommy had done.

"But Mike is a different boy when he works for me," said Ms. Wiggins. "You'll see."

Anna and Lulu were already at the hitching post with the ponies. Pam ran out to join them. She told her Pony Pals that Mike Lacey was going to help in the search.

"He won't be any help," groaned Lulu.

"He'll just pester us and get in the way," added Anna.

"But he's got a mountain bike," Pam told them. "And he knows his way around Ms. Wiggins's land."

"He'd better behave," said Lulu. "Or else."

Pam mounted Lightning and leaned forward and patted her neck. "We have to find Woolie," she told her pony. "Even if it means being nice to Mike Lacey."

Scat

Ms. Wiggins and Mike Lacey were waiting for the Pony Pals in front of the barn. Picasso was saddled up, and Mike was standing next to his bike.

Everyone said hello.

"Sorry your dog's missing," Mike told Pam.

"Thanks," said Pam. She was surprised that Mike was acting nice.

"We should decide where everyone is going to search," suggested Lulu.

Anna picked up a stick. "I'll draw a map in the dirt," she said. "Then we can divide it up."

Anna drew a big map of the property.

"I'll take the north side of Badd Brook up to the hill," said Lulu.

Anna wrote *Lulu* in that section of the map.

"And I'll take the south side of the brook," said Anna as she wrote her own name on the map.

"And I'll do the area north of the house," offered Ms. Wiggins.

Anna wrote *Ms. W* on the map.

Pam said she'd do the area northwest of the house.

Mike pointed to Lake Appamapog. "I'll go all along the lake," he said.

Pam and Lulu exchanged a glance. They were remembering when Mike and Tommy set animal traps on Ms. Wiggins's land and how they broke the law. Pam wondered if they could trust Mike.

Anna wrote *Mike* and *Pam* on the map.

Ms. Wiggins took two whistles on strings out of her pocket. She handed one to Mike and hung the other one around her neck.

Mike put on his whistle, too. "Hey, this is just like the Pony Pest whistles," he said.

The three Pony Pals glared at him.

"I mean Pony *Pals*," he said. "Sorry."

If Tommy Rand were here, thought Pam, Mike wouldn't have apologized.

"Make one long blow on the whistle to call to Woolie," said Lulu. "Two long blows if you find him and he's okay. Then everybody can meet here at the barn."

"But if he's injured or — worse," said Pam, "use the SOS signal. Three blasts of the whistle: short — long — short. We'll all go to help."

"Good plan," said Ms. Wiggins.

The search party took a last look at the map.

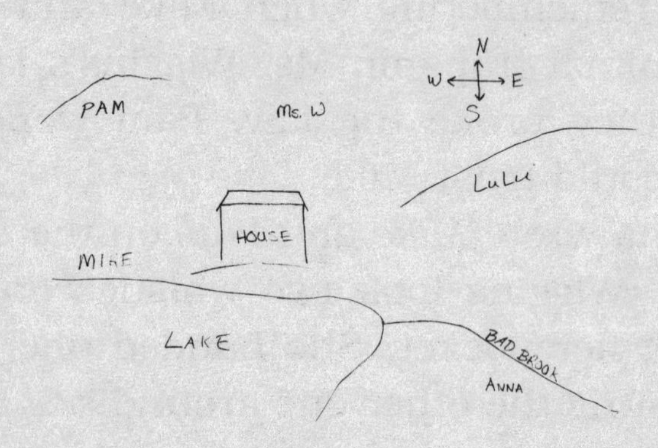

Pam mounted Lightning and turned her toward the west. "Let's go!" she shouted to the others.

Mike rode his mountain bike beside Pam and Lightning. Pam could feel Lightning tense up under her. Her pony didn't like the bike.

"Don't ride near Lightning," Pam called to Mike.

Pam thought she heard Mike say, "Sorry," but she wasn't sure. Mike burst ahead of them and made a left toward the lake.

Pam made a right onto a trail that led into the hills above the lake. She rode slowly and called Woolie's name.

"Woolie," she called. She blew her whistle. She listened. All she heard was a bunch of birds chirping in the bushes. Then she saw a flash of golden color moving between the trees. Was it Woolie? The animal stopped. A fawn and his mother stared at her for a second, then ran off. Pam was sure it was the fawn that Jack and Jill had found. Maybe Woolie's been following the fawn, thought Pam.

Suddenly, Lightning lowered her head.

Pam looked down to see what her pony smelled. It was a small pile of scat. "It's probably deer scat," she said to herself as she dismounted. Pam took a closer look. The pile looked more like dog poop than deer scat.

Lightning took another sniff. Then she raised her head and gave a loud, shrill whinny.

Lightning is calling Woolie, thought Pam.

"Do that again," she told Lightning.

Lightning threw back her head and whinnied even louder. The sound of the whinny rang through the woods.

When it died down, Pam listened. She didn't hear any answer. But Lightning's ears went forward and twitched. Lightning heard something!

Pam let Lightning's lead rope drop. "Go ahead, Lightning," she said. "Go find Woolie."

Lightning turned to the left and walked onto a small trail.

Pam followed her.

Lightning whinnied.

Pam heard a faraway bark answer the whinny.

Woolie was answering Lightning! "Hurry, Lightning!" Pam told her pony. "Let's go find him."

Pam and Lightning ran along the trail. Pam heard Woolie's bark again. It was still far away. Pam's heart sank. Woolie wasn't running to meet them. Something was wrong.

"We're coming, Woolie!" Pam shouted at the top of her lungs. "We'll find you."

As Lightning and Pam continued along the narrow trail, bushes scratched Pam's arms. But she didn't care. She was finding Woolie. She would help him.

The barking was louder and louder. Lightning suddenly turned to her right and squeezed between bushes on the side of the trail.

When Lightning was on the other side of the bushes, she nickered a sad little sound.

Pam pushed through the bushes, too. She saw what made Lightning sad.

There, lying in the dirt, was Woolie. The fur on his leg was matted with blood. A big steel trap held him down.

"Oh, Woolie," cried Pam.

Woolie looked up, bared his teeth, and growled. He's frightened and injured, thought Pam. And he's angry with me.

Pam put her whistle to her mouth and blew the SOS signal two times. Short — long — short. Short — long — short.

Woolie needed help. And fast.

A Licking

Pam noticed that the blood on Woolie's leg was dried. He must have been trapped for a long time, thought Pam. Maybe since the morning.

Woolie growled at her again.

Pam knew that a trapped or injured dog can be dangerous. Woolie was trapped *and* injured. But he needed help.

"Woolie," Pam said in a calm voice, "it's only me. I want to help you. I have to look at the trap."

How can I get close to him? wondered Pam. She remembered that she had his water bowl with her. He must be thirsty, she thought. If he has some water, maybe he'll calm down. Then I can look at his leg and the trap.

Pam took a bottle of water and the bowl out of her saddlebag. While she was pouring the water, Lightning moved closer to Woolie.

Woolie is so upset, thought Pam, he might bite Lightning. But it was too late to stop Lightning. Pam's pony was already bending over Woolie. Lightning whinnied softly as if to say, "I'm sorry this happened to you."

Woolie whimpered a sad little dog noise. He was calm now.

Pam placed the water where Woolie could easily drink it. Woolie lapped up the water gratefully.

While he drank, Pam studied the trap. She couldn't figure out how to release it. She wanted to try, but what if she did it wrong? She might hurt Woolie even more.

Woolie whimpered again. Pam brushed the hair out of his eyes. Her dog looked so sad and frightened.

"Poor Woolie," said Pam. "We have to get you out of that trap."

Pam heard a whistle blast. Someone was coming to help her! She hoped that it was Lulu. Lulu might know how to spring the trap.

Pam blew her whistle again.

"I'm coming," answered a voice in the woods.

It wasn't Lulu's voice. It was a boy's voice.

Mike Lacey pushed his bike into the small clearing. "What happened to Woolie?" he asked.

Pam jumped to her feet and put her hands on her hips. "He's caught in a trap," she said. "See what your stupid traps do, Mike Lacey?"

Mike squatted down next to Woolie. "I didn't set this trap," he said. "I don't do that anymore. I help Ms. Wiggins find traps, so the animals aren't hurt." He patted Woolie on the head. "I'm sorry that I didn't find this one, Woolie," he said.

Mike knows a lot about traps, thought Pam. Maybe he can help Woolie.

"Can you get that trap off Woolie?" she asked him.

Mike studied the trap. "I haven't seen a trap like this one before," he said. "But I can try."

Pam knelt on the other side of Woolie. "If you make a mistake, could you hurt him more?" she asked.

"I'll be careful," Mike told her. "Can you hold him still?"

Pam nodded. "I had to do that when my dad took porcupine quills out of his nose."

"Poor Woolie," said Mike. "That must have hurt."

"Woolie's been through a lot," said Pam. "I hope his leg isn't broken."

Mike looked carefully at the trap. "I think I know how it works," he said. "I'll count to three when it's time."

Pam put her hands on Woolie's haunches.

"You are such a good dog," she said. Woolie looked up at her. She looked back into his big brown eyes. He totally trusts me, she thought. I was mean to him. He's been away for two days. He's caught in a trap. And he still trusts me.

"One," Mike counted. "Two. Three. Open."

Mike pulled on the trap with all his might. The trap opened.

Woolie pulled his leg away. He was free.

"You did it, Mike!" exclaimed Pam.

Woolie was wiggling like crazy. He wanted to get up.

"Stay still, Woolie," said Pam. "I have to clean off your leg and see if it's broken."

Pam asked Mike to hold Woolie while she got her first aid kit out of the saddlebag.

Whistles sounded from three different parts of the woods. "They're all looking for us," Pam told Mike.

She blew her whistle to signal where they were.

Mike kept Woolie still while Pam cleaned the dried blood off his leg. She found the cut.

It was long, but not deep. “My dad will have to look at this,” Pam told Mike. She ran her hand along Woolie’s leg.

“I don’t think he broke any bones,” she said.

Just then, Woolie wiggled out of Mike’s arms.

“Woolie,” called Pam. “Stay!”

But it was too late. Woolie was running around the clearing and yapping excitedly. Pam was afraid that he’d run away again. But he didn’t. Woolie was just happy to be free from the trap.

“I guess he *didn’t* break any bones,” said Mike with a laugh.

Lulu and Anna came into the clearing with their ponies. Woolie ran over to them.

“He was in a trap,” Pam told her friends. But no one was listening to her. They were all shouting excitedly and playing with Woolie.

Ms. Wiggins and Picasso joined the happy group.

Finally, everyone quieted down. Ms. Wiggins and Lulu checked Woolie's leg, too.

"You're lucky that Woolie stayed still when he was in the trap," said Lulu. "It could have been a lot worse."

"I know," said Pam.

Woolie was barking and running around the three ponies and Picasso.

"Woolie's back to his old tricks," said Anna with a laugh.

Pam thought about all the adventures Woolie must have had. She knew he visited the Quinns. And that he had dinner and stayed the night at a farm. But what else did he do? Did he try to track the fawn and his mother? Did he try to go home and become lost? Or was he running away? Pam would never know the whole story. She was just glad that Woolie was safe and with her again.

She squatted down and called, "Woolie, come here."

Woolie turned at the sound of her voice and ran over to her.

She put her arms around him. "I'm sorry I

yelled at you yesterday," she said. "I love you, Woolie."

Woolie looked up and licked Pam's face. She felt a nibble on the top of her head. It was Lightning.

Pam reached up and put an arm around Lightning's neck. "You found Woolie," she told her pony. "Thank you. I love you both so much."

Ms. Wiggins, Lulu, Anna, and Mike were watching Pam with her dog and pony. They were all smiling. Even Mike Lacey.

"Thanks!" she told them all. "Thank you for helping me find Woolie."

Dear Reader,

I am having fun researching and writing the Pony Pal books. I've met great kids and wonderful ponies at homes, farms, and riding schools. Some of my ideas for Pony Pal adventures have even come from these visits!

I remember the day I made up the main characters for the series. I was walking on a country road in New England. First, I decided that the three girls would be smart, independent, and kind. Then I gave them their names—Pam, Anna, and Lulu. (Look at the initial of each girl's name. See what it spells when you put them together!) Later, I created the three ponies. When I reached home, I turned on my computer and started to write. And I haven't stopped since!

My friends say that I am a little bit like all of the Pony Pals. I am very organized, like Pam. I love nature, like Lulu. But I think that I am most like Anna. I am dyslexic and a good artist, just like her.

Readers often wonder about my life. I live in an apartment in New York City near Central Park and the Museum of Natural History. I enjoy swimming, hiking, painting, and reading. I also love to make up stories. I have been writing novels for children and young adults for more than twenty years! Several of my books have won the Children's Choice Award.

Many Pony Pal readers send me letters, drawings, and photos. I tape them to the wall in my office. They inspire me to write more Pony Pal stories. Thank you very much!

I don't ride anymore and I've never had a pony. But you don't have to ride to love ponies! And you certainly don't need a pony to be a Pony Pal.

Happy Reading,

Jeanne Betancourt